Dear Parent:
Your child's love of reading starts here!

Every child learns to read in a different way and at his or her own speed. Some go back and forth between reading levels and read favorite books again and again. Others read through each level in order. You can help your young reader improve and become more confident by encouraging his or her own interests and abilities. From books your child reads with you to the first books he or she reads alone, there are I Can Read Books for every stage of reading:

SHARED READING
Basic language, word repetition, and whimsical illustrations, ideal for sharing with your emergent reader

BEGINNING READING
Short sentences, familiar words, and simple concepts for children eager to read on their own

READING WITH HELP
Engaging stories, longer sentences, and language play for developing readers

READING ALONE
Complex plots, challenging vocabulary, and high-interest topics for the independent reader

ADVANCED READING
Short paragraphs, chapters, and exciting themes for the perfect bridge to chapter books

I Can Read Books have introduced children to the joy of reading since 1957. Featuring award-winning authors and illustrators and a fabulous cast of beloved characters, I Can Read Books set the standard for beginning readers.

A lifetime of discovery begins with the magical words **"I Can Read!"**

Visit www.icanread.com for information
on enriching your child's reading experience.

For Justin Burrows
and his zeal for
transforming his
own mighty truck
—C.B.

To Gubbles!
—T.C.

Clarence was just a muddy pickup.

One day, there was a big storm.

Lightning zapped the car wash.

Now Clarence has a secret.

Water turns him into Mighty Truck!

I Can Read Book® is a trademark of HarperCollins Publishers.

Mighty Truck: Surf's Up! Copyright © 2019 by HarperCollins Publishers
All rights reserved. Manufactured in China. No part of this book may be used or reproduced in any manner whatsoever without written permission except in the case of brief quotations embodied in critical articles and reviews. For information address HarperCollins Children's Books, a division of HarperCollins Publishers, 195 Broadway, New York, NY 10007.
www.icanread.com

Library of Congress Control Number: 2018941366
ISBN: 978-0-06-234476-2 (trade bg.)—ISBN: 978-0-06-234475-5 (pbk.)

Book design by Celeste Knudsen
18 19 20 21 22 SCP 10 9 8 7 6 5 4 3 2 1 ❖ First Edition

MIGHTY TRUCK

SURF'S UP!

BY CHRIS BARTON   ILLUSTRATED BY TROY CUMMINGS

An Imprint of HarperCollinsPublishers

Mr. Dent was a surf wagon.

He lived next door to Clarence.

Clarence saw Mr. Dent every day.

He saw Mr. Dent's cat less often.

Mr. Dent's cat, Throttle, hid a lot.

One day, the weather was perfect.

It was perfect for the beach.

"Good morning," Clarence said.

"Will you catch some waves today?"

"You know us!" Mr. Dent said.

"We would hate to miss out on those.

Am I right, little dude?"

Mr. Dent winked at Throttle.

"Meow," said Throttle.

That meow meant something.

It did not mean "You are right!"

It meant, "I do not like the water."

Mr. Dent did not know

that Throttle hated water.

"Told you," he said to Clarence.

"Do you want to join us for a bit?"

Clarence liked that idea.

"Sure," he replied.

"The beach sounds fun.

But I will just watch.

I never learned how to surf."

BEACH

"Same here," Mr. Dent said.

"I will watch with you."

"I'm confused," said Clarence.

"You sure *sound* like a surfer."

12

"No, I can't surf," Mr. Dent said.

"Dude, I just talk this way.

I'm here to support my cat.

Throttle *loves* to surf."

Throttle did not love to surf.

Mr. Dent was mistaken.

But Throttle could not tell him.

Not with words, anyway.

"Meow," said Throttle.

It meant, "Please, not again."

Mr. Dent did not know that.

"Have fun!" replied Mr. Dent.

"Will he be OK?" Clarence asked.

"Totally!" said Mr. Dent.

"Meow," said Throttle.

Throttle was not OK.

There was a strong current.

The current carried the cat away.

Throttle was in trouble.

Clarence knew what he had to do.

Clarence found two pieces of wood.

He floated out toward Throttle.

It took a long while.

Clarence finally got there.

Throttle was not alone anymore.

But then a giant wave came along.

Clarence and Throttle saw it.

Then they were nearly under it.

The salty spray covered Throttle.

He turned into a wet, unhappy cat.

The spray got Clarence wet, too.

Clarence turned into Mighty Truck.

Throttle was surprised.

"All right!" said Mighty Truck.

"Let's go!

Hold on tight!

Back to shore we'll . . . WHOA!"

One of the boards floated away.

"Now what?" said Mighty Truck.

"Meow," said Throttle.

"Great idea!" said Mighty Truck.

"Maybe we can windsurf!"

Throttle did not argue.

"Watch this," said Mighty Truck.

He opened his tailgate.

"It's not just a tailgate," he said.

"Now it's a *sail*gate!"

Mighty Truck caught the breeze.

Or the breeze caught him.

Truck and cat rode fast on the wind.

They roared past the shoreline.

They rushed beyond Mr. Dent.

Then they skidded on the beach.

Mighty Truck and Throttle tumbled.

And tumbled.

And tumbled.

They rolled tail over tailpipe.

Finally, they stopped.

The sand had changed Mighty Truck.

He had turned back into Clarence.

"Dude!" Mr. Dent said to Clarence.

"You must have wiped out!"

"Did I miss much?" Clarence asked.

"Only Mighty Truck!" Mr. Dent said.

"He saved my cat!"

"Sorry I missed him," Clarence said.

Clarence looked at Throttle.

Throttle looked at Clarence.

"That was fun," Clarence said.

"Should we do it again, Throttle?"

"Purr," said the cat.

That purr meant something.

It meant, "Anytime, Mighty Truck."